by TOM K. RYAN

FAWCETT GOLD MEDAL • NEW YORK

Library of Congress Catalog Card Number: 86-91830

ISBN 0-449-13244-7

Manufactured in the United States of America

First Edition: June 1987

10 9 8 7 6 5 4 3 2 1

SCRIBBLE
SCRIBBLE
SCRIBBLE

RIP!

KEEP YOUR EYES ON ME! IF I RAISE MY LANCE, YOU ATTACK!

WHEN I RAISE MY SHIELD, RETREAT!

AND IF I RAISE BOTH, IGNORE IT— I'M AN INCURABLE PRACTICAL JOKER!

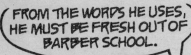

THE LATEST ISSUE OF YOUR GOOD CRYPTKEEPING MAG'S HERE, WIMBLE!

CLAUDE CLAY
UNDERTAKER
YOU PLUG 'EM—I PLANT 'EM

IT'S THE ANNUAL FASHION ISSUE!

BRING IT TO ME, PLEASE!

I'M DYING TO SEE THE NEW NIGHT CRAWLER PRINT SMOCK WITH THE MUSHROOM BUTTONS.

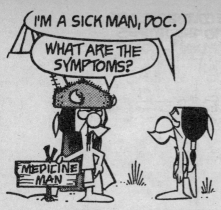

WHAT ARE YOU READING, LIMPID LIZARD?

INSTRUCTSHUNS.

" TO OPERATE, GRASP HANDLE (A) IN HAND (B) AND MOVE UPWARD AN' KLOCKWISE."

HMM.. THIS NEW TOMMYHAWK'S A LOT LIKE MY OLD WUN.

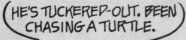

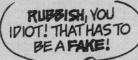

A THRILLER CALLED "BRET HARDY AND THE RANCH OF THE SPORTSMAN VAMPIRE!"